DISCARD

How to Teach a  lug to Read

Susan Pearson

illustrated by
David Slonim

Marshall Cavendish Children

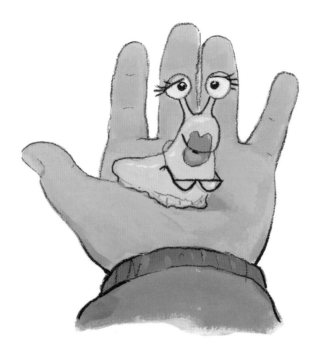

Marshall Cavendish Corporation, 99 White Plains Road, Tarrytown, NY 10591
www.marshallcavendish.us/kids

Library of Congress Cataloging-in-Publication Data
Pearson, Susan.
How to teach a slug to read / by Susan Pearson ; illustrated by David Slonim. — 1st ed.
p. cm.
Summary: Provides simple, step-by-step instructions for teaching a slug how to read, including using Mother Slug rhymes,
helping your slug sound out words, and making vocabulary lists.
ISBN 978-0-7614-5805-0
[1. Reading—Fiction. 2. Slugs (Mollusks)—Fiction.] I. Slonim, David, ill. II. Title.
PZ7.P323316How 2011
[E]—dc22
2010024289

The illustrations are rendered in acrylic and charcoal on illustration board.
Book design by Anahid Hamparian
Editor: Margery Cuyler

Printed in China [E]
First edition
1 3 5 6 4 2

When you teach a slug to read, you should:
1. Start out by putting labels on his favorite things.

2. Next, find a really good book. This is very important or your slug will lose interest. The best books will have some slugs in them.

Mother Slug rhymes are good. They have *lots* of slugs in them, and the rhymes will help your slug remember the words.

ttle slug,
smooth as silk,
him in a satin shirt,
bread and milk.

4. Find a rock for your slug to sit on so he can see the page better. Be patient. It will take your slug some time to climb up on the rock.

Mary had a little slug,
His skin was smooth as silk,
She dressed him in a satin shirt,
And fed him bread and milk.

5. Show your slug the words that repeat a lot. This will help him spot them right away.

learned to fly fly fly.
Say good-bye bye bye.

6. Help your slug sound out words.

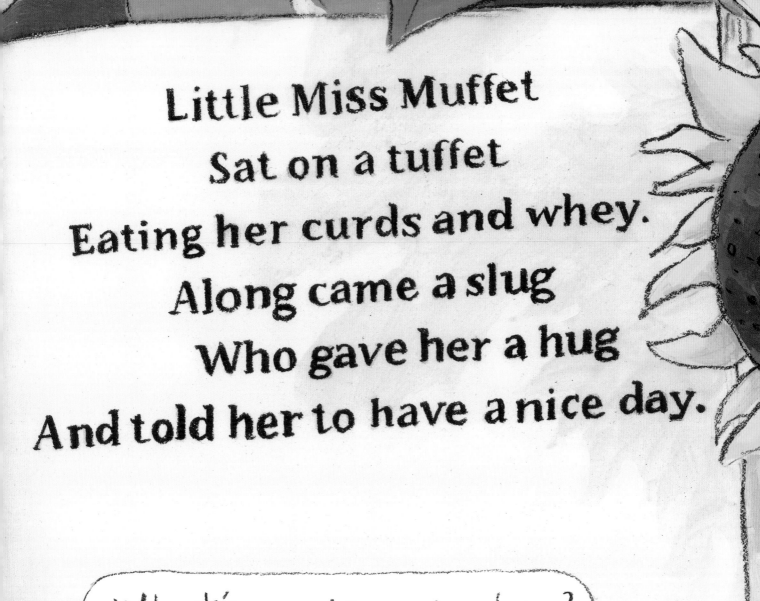

Little Miss Muffet
Sat on a tuffet
Eating her curds and whey.
Along came a slug
Who gave her a hug
And told her to have a nice day.

What's curds and whey?

Cottage cheese.

No kidding!

Sweet Sammy Slug
Slides through the town
Upstairs and downstairs

In his nightgown

To make sure that children
Are tucked in their beds
And dreams of slug fairies
Dance in their heads.

9. Read your slug's favorite poems with him as many times as he wants. Read him other books too!

THE SNAIL IN THE HAT
Go Slug, Go!
Ha Ha!
to where the wild slugs are.

10. Be patient. Reading isn't learned in a day.
It can take months. But don't give up—
it's worth it in the end.

And then, one day, he will read books to you!

Then he will read books to the beetles and the butterflies and the grasshoppers and the crickets and the bumblebees and the dragonflies. He may start a story hour or even a school.

Once upon a slime
when all were sleeping
a slug came creeping

Books will teach him how to play slug soccer.

Books will show him slugs in other lands.

Books will show him the whole wide world.

And all because YOU taught your slug to read!